To Griffith and Graham, the two little boys I read *Goodnight Moon* to over and over and over.

—L.L.

Good Day, Good Night

For information address HarperCollins Children's Books, a division of HarperCollins Publishers, 195 Broadway, New York, NY 10007.
www.harpercollinschildrens.com

ISBN 978-0-06-238310-5 — 978-0-06-269379-2 (special edition)

The artist used acrylics on illustration board to create the illustrations for this book.
Typography by Jeanne L. Hogle
17 18 19 20 21 SCP 10 9 8 7 6 5 4 3 2 1
❖
First Edition

Good Day, Good Night

By MARGARET WISE BROWN
Pictures by LOREN LONG

HARPER
An Imprint of HarperCollins*Publishers*

When the sun came up the day began.
Who saw the first light of the sun?
"I," said a bunny, "the only one."

Good morning, world!

Hello, daylight

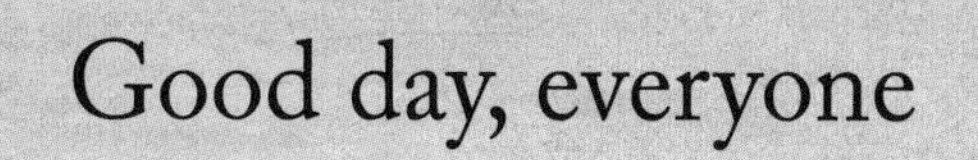

Good day, everyone

Good-bye, night

Good day, trees
And birds in the skies

Good day, bees
Buzz out of your hives

Good day, kitty
There's milk in your cup

Stretch, little cat
Try to wake up

Good morning to you!
Open your eyes
For every day
Is a new surprise

Go live your day!

When the moon came up the night began.

Good night, birds
Down in your nest

Good night, bees
Time to rest

Good night, sky
And the daylight
Good night, flowers
Bugs, good night

The Harey Dairy

Good night, kitty
Good night, bear

Good night, people
everywhere

Good night, toys
Good night, world
Under the covers
I cuddle and curl

b
B

The rabbit twitched his nose
And his ruby eyes closed
Good night, little bunny
Go to sleep.